Penny Jo's Magnificent Toes

Written by Mark Eischen

Illustrated by Erica Landers
Layout by Douglas Spossey

Copyright Mark Eischen - 2016
ISBN-13: 978-1530408382
ISBN - 10: 1530408385

For Jane and Abbie

Penny Jo woke up on a very big day
    In the very same place she wanted to stay.

She thought of excuses to stay home instead
    And stared at her toes at the end of her bed.

She wondered if maybe she stayed extra quiet
    they'd forget her doorknob and not even try it.

he sat up and thought, "I am NOT wearing stockings..."
   When Polly burst in, without even knocking.

Mom, she's still in her jammies and she hardly seems ready!"
   Penny Jo wished Polly had left already.

But today was the biggest day of the year.
    A day to whoop and holler and cheer.

A day to be your most porcupiniest!
    From her big brother Paul, to yes, Polly (the tiniest).

The sun was up when they got to the square
    Most of the families were already there.

Mayor Mc Doogle climbed up on his stump.
    He shook out his quills from his head to his rump.

He cleared his throat as Mayors will do…
    "Welcome to the Annual Hullaballoo!"

They struck up the band and began the parade
    Penny Jo found a small place in the shade.

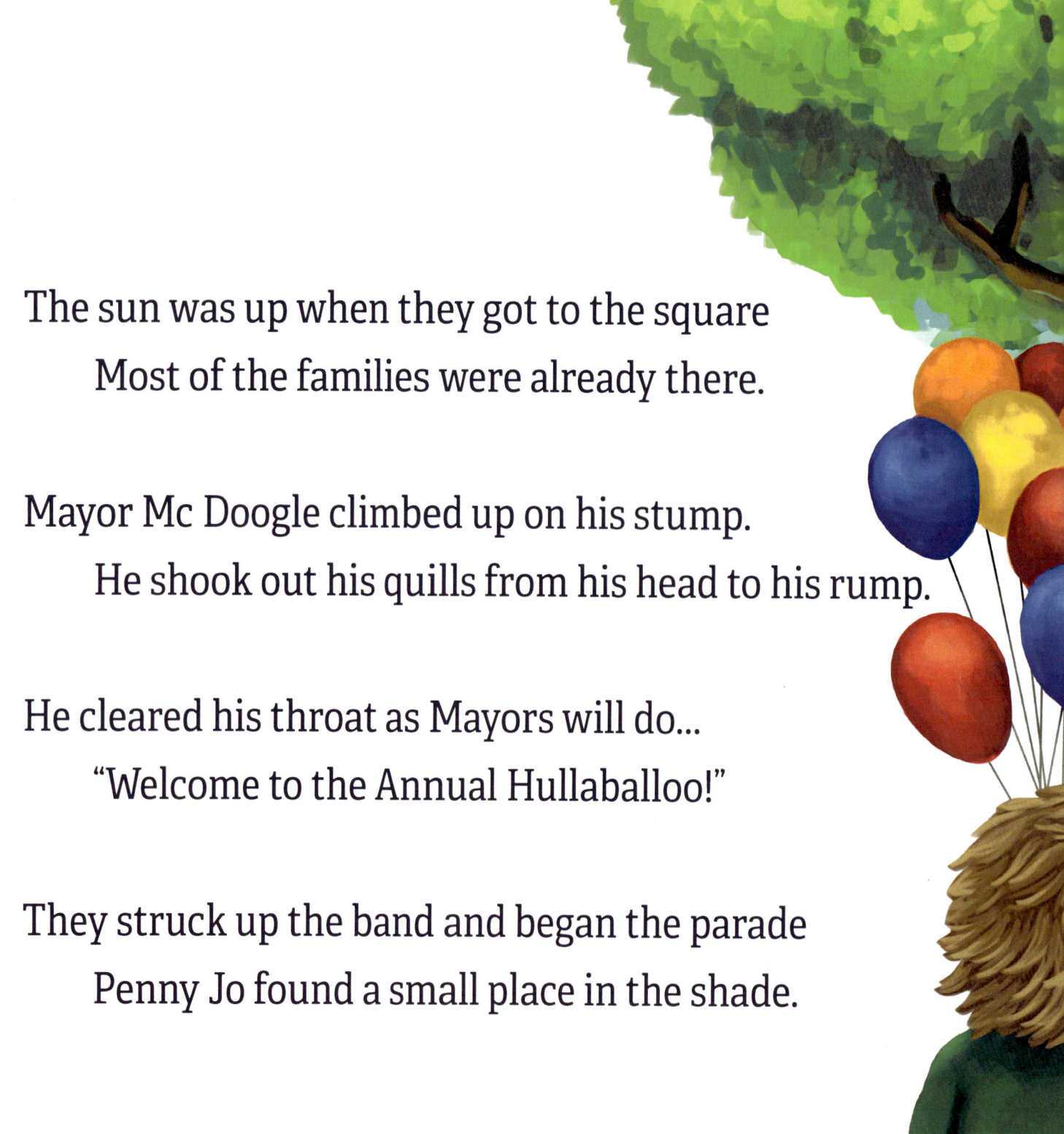

The other kids picked teams for target practice.
   Penny Jo plopped down and felt more like a cactus.

She didn't raise her hand. She didn't get all excited.
   And she didn't even care if she wasn't invited.

See there really is no nice way to say...
    Penny Jo's quills kind of bent a strange way.

Though her mom tried to straighten them nightly...
    She'd look and say, "Hmmm... still rather unsightly."

Where other kids' coats were shiny and nice
    Penny Jo's made strangers stop and look twice.

Mean kids would sometimes tease her and such.
    Penny Jo didn't care. At least not very much.

"Big deal... nice quills. Everyone's got em".
 She rolled back in the grass on her porcupine bottom.

"I hope nobody comes back for hours..."
 She wrapped her eight toes around six yellow flowers.

She opened her eyes when she felt a slight breeze
    To a big ball of colors floating up through the trees!

It was a giant balloon... and below it a basket.
    "Where are you going?" She wanted to ask it.

Then a MONKEY leaned over and threw out a rope!

"Well, grab on Penny Jo! Don't just lay there and mope... You're a born trapeezer! It's quite plain to see!"

"Ummm... there must be some mistake." She said. "Why choose me?"

"Why, just take one look at those wonderful paws! Those perfect round pads... those fabulous claws! Why NOT choose you? You hardly could blame us. We knew right away. You should be rich and famous!"

Penny Jo wasn't sure what she should do.

Except probably go back to the Hullaballoo.

Then she pictured the other kids, laughing and gloating...

She grabbed on with both feet
   And WHOOSH She was floating!

"Welcome aboard! What a day for a ride!"
The Monkey called out over the side.
"But I've never even tried trapeezing before"
She said, as she flew past the General Store.

"Well, we could drop you
back at the very same place."

"Go higher!" She said,
a big smile on her face.

Penny Jo never thought she would find herself flying.
 But she didn't feel scared and she sure wasn't crying

"I guess I could try a couple of swings…"
 "Well, alright then! Meet my Iguana. He sings!"

Penny Jo swung high, out past the balloon...
   The Iguana broke into a country tune.

Just when it seemed a little too late...
   Penny Jo let go and did a nice figure eight.

The whole Hullabaloo was pointing and clapping...
  The Monkey was dancing, his fingers were snapping.

She grabbed back hold after two perfect twists.
  The Iguana was dancing and pumping his fists.

She did triple quadruples with full tummy tucks.
She did long free falls, into last second ducks.

The crowd swooned when she went into her dives.
They'd never seen such a show in all of their lives!

Penny Jo kept flying as day turned to night
And everyone agreed the most beautiful sight

Was the sun setting slowly over the hills,
shining just right on Penny Jo's perfect quills.

I hope Penny Jo's story might just remind you.
That someday your Monkey and Iguana will find you.

Even if you don't see them some days...
There are so many people you'll inspire and amaze.

Be aware of the ropes that will drift past your toes.
When one does, grab on tight...
and see where it goes.

Made in United States
North Haven, CT
13 October 2025